Anybody Can Play

by Jocelyn Stevenson

Illustrated by Beverly Phillips

Featuring Jim Henson's Sesame Street Muppets

A SESAME STREET/GOLDEN PRESS BOOK
Published by Western Publishing Company, Inc.
in conjunction with Children's Television Workshop.

One rainy day on Sesame Street Bert
couldn't think of anything to do.
He had already counted his paper clips
and bottle caps and read his favorite pigeon
book again.

Ernie came in out of the rain, soaking wet.
"What a day!" he said.

"Hhhhhhhhheeeeehhh," sighed Bert.

"Gee, Bert, old buddy. What's wrong?" Ernie
asked.

"I just wish it weren't raining so I could go
outside," said Bert.

"But, Bert, there are lots of things you can do inside," said Ernie. He ran into the bedroom and came back with a big box.

"Here's your bowling ball, Bert," he said. "You can count the holes in it!"

"Thanks, but no thanks," said Bert.

"Then what about wearing this funny mask?" asked Ernie.

"What's so funny about that?" said Bert glumly.

"I know what you can do, Bert. You can think about things — like penguins or tubas or elevators!"

"But that's what I've been doing, Ernie,
and it's boring." Bert sighed again, and sat
down by the window.
   "I don't have anything to do but twiddle
my thumbs."

"What's wrong with that, Bert?" asked Ernie.
He put his thumbs in his ears and waggled his
fingers. "And there are other nifty things you can
do with your hands."

"I can't think of a thing," said Bert, putting
his hands in his pockets.

"Then watch this,"
said Ernie, clapping his
hands above his head.
Bert clapped his hands
three times and stopped.
"Forget it," he said.

"But you haven't tried the good stuff
yet," cried Ernie. "What about this?"
He made a butterfly with his hands.

"Or this?" He rubbed his head
with one hand and patted his stomach
with the other. Bert just
kept his hands in
his pockets.

"There are games we can play
with other parts of the body,
Bert. Let's try arms!"
Ernie said cheerfully.
    First he made big circles
with his arms.

"We can swim, Bert!" he said,
and he "swam" around the room.

"I don't know how to swim,"
said Bert.
    "Come on, Bert, old buddy,
try this!" Ernie touched
his elbows together.

"Or this!" He flapped
his arms like a chicken.

"Or this!" He clasped
his hands over his head
like a champion.

"That's no fun," said Bert.
"I wish I could go outside."

"It's still raining, Bert," said Ernie. "So let's do legs."
Ernie hopped and skipped. Then he walked
like a pigeon. Bert just watched.

"Hey, Bert," Ernie said. "Let's march."

Bert looked down at his legs. Slowly, little
by little, he started to march with Ernie. First
he marched with very tiny steps. Then he lifted
his knees higher and higher. The more Bert
marched, the more he liked it.

"Now let's do feet!" said Ernie, taking off
his sneakers and wiggling his toes. Bert took off
his saddle shoes and wiggled his toes, too.

Then Ernie grabbed a crayon with his toes
and drew a picture. So did Bert.

"Now let's use our heads," said Ernie.
Ernie and Bert shook their heads and
nodded their heads.

Ernie looked up, up, up.
Bert looked down, down, down.

They rolled their heads in circles.

Then they stopped to think. "What are you
thinking about, Bert?" asked Ernie.

"I'm thinking about what to do next," said Bert.
"Let's do shoulders!" Bert lifted up his shoulders
until they almost touched his ears. Ernie put
his shoulders down.

Bert put his shoulders back.
Ernie put his shoulders forward.

"That's keen!" Bert said, and he began to walk
around the room moving his shoulders backward and
forward. "It's like marching
with your shoulders!"

"Hey, Bert," said Ernie, "it's time for ribs. Put your hands on your sides and feel your ribs go in and out when you breathe."

"You're right!" Bert cried. "That's more fun than a flock of pigeons. What else can I do with my ribs?"

"You can count them," said Ernie.

So Bert counted his ribs. "What else, Ernie? What else are ribs for?" he asked.

"Well, Bert old buddy," Ernie said.
"Ribs can be . . . TICKLED!"
And he tickled Bert's ribs
until Bert couldn't help laughing.

"What's next?" gasped Bert.
"We can do backs," Ernie said.
"What in the world can I do
with my back, Ernie?" Bert asked.

"I don't know, Bert. I'll rest while
you give it a try."
So Bert bent his back and then
he touched his toes. He leaned to
one side, and then to the other.

Then he started to twist from side
to side. "Come on, Ernie," he said,
"don't just sit there. Let's do the twist!"

"Hot dog! Let's do the whole
body now, Ernie," said Bert.
"Look! I can be a bird...

...or an elephant...

…or a frog…

…or a snake! This is really
fun, Ernie!"
 But Ernie was too tired
to play any more.

Bert began leaping around the room,
dancing and turning somersaults.
Ernie looked out the window.

"Hey, Bert," he said.
"Guess what. It's stopped
raining. Now we can go outside!"

"Not now, Ernie," said Bert.
"I still have to do my wrists."

Ernie went outside and sat on the stoop
in the sun. "I know something else that my body
can do," he said. "It's called resting." And he fell
fast asleep.

ABCDEFGHIJKL